For Jess, Louise, and Ella—
the most stylish girls in town

Copyright © 1999 by Niki Daly
By arrangement with The Inkman, Cape Town, South Africa
Hand-lettering by Andrew van der Merwe
All rights reserved
First published in Great Britain by Frances Lincoln Limited, 1999
Printed in China
First American edition, 1999
Sunburst edition, 2004
1 3 5 7 9 10 8 6 4 2

Library of Congress Cataloging-in-Publication Data
Daly, Niki.
   Jamela's dress / Niki Daly.
      p.   cm.
   Summary: Jamela gets in trouble when she takes the material intended
for a new dress for Mama, parades it in the street, and allows it to become
dirty and torn.
   ISBN: 0-374-43720-3 (pbk.)
   [1. Clothing and dress—Fiction.   2. Blacks—South Africa—Fiction.
3. South Africa—Fiction.]   I. Title.

PZ7.D1715 Jam 1999
[E]—dc21   98-42048

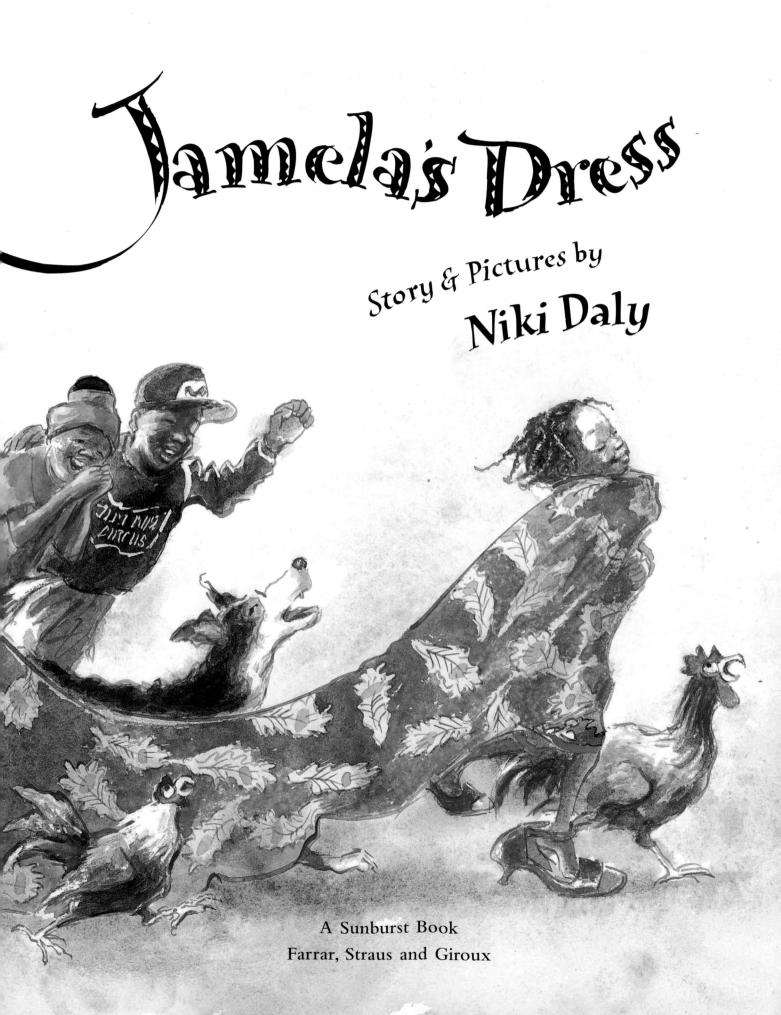

Jamela's Dress

Story & Pictures by
Niki Daly

A Sunburst Book
Farrar, Straus and Giroux

Mama was very pleased with the new material she'd found at Mnandi's. She had worked hard to earn the money for it.

"It's beautiful, Mama," said Jamela, stroking the crisp new material.

"Yes, it's beautiful. It costs a lot of money—but I need something special to wear for Thelma's wedding," said Mama.

Jamela helped Mama wash the stiffness out of the new material. Together they hung it up to dry.

"I'll look after it, Mama," said Jamela.

"Thank you," said Mama. "Just make sure Taxi doesn't jump up and dirty my material."

"Okay," said Jamela.

A warm breeze blew. Jamela rubbed her cheek against the soft material and followed the beautiful patterns with her finger.

When Taxi barked, Mama called, "Jamela, are you looking after my material?"

"Yes, Mama. It's getting nice and dry," said Jamela.

Dreamily, Jamela swayed between the folds of material as they flapped and wrapped around her into a dress.

When Mama heard nothing going on, she called,
"Are you looking after my material, Jamela?"
There was no answer.

Down the road went Jamela, proud as a peacock,
to show Thelma her beautiful dress for the wedding.

She passed Miss Style hairdressers and the Snak-Pak grocery.
"Hi, beautiful!" called old Greasy Hands, who was fixing up
Thelma's wedding car.

Children sang,

Kwela Jamela African Queen!

Taxi barked, and Mrs. Zibi's chicken went wild.

Then a boy on a bicycle, who wasn't looking where he was going, went skidding all over Mama's dress material.

What a show!

In his photo studio, Archie heard the commotion.
He ran out, clutching his special camera, and shouted,
"Hold it, Jamela!"

So Jamela posed. The children pushed in. Taxi
pushed in. Mrs. Zibi and her chicken pushed in.
And the boy on the bicycle just s-q-u-e-e-z-e-d in.
They all smiled.

But when Thelma saw Jamela, she scolded, "Haai, Jamela! Your mama's going to be *verrrry* upset when she sees what you've done with her material."

And Mama was. Mama was so upset that she couldn't even look
at Jamela. She just looked at the dirty, torn material and said sadly,
"What am I going to wear for the wedding?"

Everyone felt sorry for Mama and cross with Jamela. Even Jamela
was cross with Jamela. She hadn't meant to ruin Mama's material.
It just happened.

A few days later, Archie saw Jamela coming down the road without her usual smile. He called, "Hey, Jamela, why so sad? Come see the good news." Pointing to a front-page photograph in the newspaper, Archie read proudly:

"KWELA JAMELA
AFRICAN QUEEN—
*a prize-winning photograph
taken by Archie Khumalo.*"

But instead of looking happy, Jamela started to cry—and she told Archie all about Mama's messed-up material.

"That's a sad, sad story, Jamela," said Archie, "but it has a happy ending." He put his hand into his bag. Jamela wiped her eyes.

"See," said Archie, taking out a bundle of money. "I won big bucks for that photograph."

Jamela had never seen so much money.

"You can buy lots of things at the shops with that money, Archie," said Jamela.

"Right!" Archie laughed. "That's the happy ending."

In the afternoon, Archie arrived carrying a gift for Jamela's mama.

"What is this, Archie?" Mama asked in surprise.

"Open it, Mama, open it!" cried Jamela.

Mama unwrapped the parcel. Inside was a beautiful piece of material from Mnandi's—just like the first piece.

Jamela jumped up and down.

"*Enkosi kakhulu*. Thank you, Archie!" said Mama.

"No, you must thank Kwela Jamela African Queen,"
said Archie, holding up his prize-winning photograph.

When Mama saw it, she gave Jamela a big hug.

After Archie had gone, Jamela helped Mama
wash the material and hang it up to dry.
"It's the most beautiful material in
the world," said Jamela.
Mama just smiled.
They sang songs as they
watched the feathery patterns
dance in the warm breeze.

Then Mama and Jamela played
a hand-clapping game
for a while.

"Let's do teapots, Mama!" cried Jamela.
So Jamela taught Mama to do
a little song
about a teapot
with a spout.
They dipped
and tipped
and the tea
poured out.

When they stopped, the material felt warm and
dry. So Mama showed Jamela how to fold it—just as
she had learned to do it when she was a little girl.

That evening, Mama cut and sewed until she had her special dress to wear to Thelma's wedding. When she finished, there was a piece of material left over.

Mama measured it with her eye, this way and that way. Then she looked at sleeping Jamela and smiled.

The hands of the clock passed midnight, and Mama was
still hard at work. Every now and then she sang softly
to herself, "Kwela Jamela African Queen."

Next day at the wedding, Thelma looked radiant.

Mama looked lovely,

and when Archie said, "Smile, everyone!"
guess who had the biggest smile?

Kwela Jamela African Queen!

—that's who!

AUTHOR'S NOTE

As a schoolboy in the 1960s, I remember being caught up in the vibrant penny-whistle music played on the streets of Cape Town. The musicians, not much older than myself, made brilliant music called "kwela." The word comes from the Nguni word *khwela*, meaning "to start," as well as "to climb on," "to get moving."

Calling "Kwela!" was the signal of the leader of the penny-whistle group to start playing. That's how the music got its name. Unhappily, in those days of Apartheid, "Kwela-kwela!" was also the warning cry on the streets whenever a police van was sighted. These vans were known as "kwela-kwela vans," reflecting the other meanings of the original word.

Now, in the new South Africa, when "Kwela-kwela!" is heard, it is the happy call of taxi drivers as they hurry their passengers on board the busy "kwela taxis"—so the word has come to represent action and excitement.